SEEING
CARTER

D1368435

SEEING CARTER

Leah Shepherd

To order additional copies of this book, contact:
Xlibris
1-888-795-4274
www.Xlibris.com
Orders@Xlibris.com
808063

*Dedicated with much love to Grant and Ben, who
I cherish every day with all my heart*

ACKNOWLEDGEMENTS

First, I want to thank my parents, Bob and Gigi Carlson. This book would not be possible without their support and encouragement over many years. Heartfelt thanks to my very supportive, loving, and patient husband Scott, who is better than the sunrise and sunset combined. Thanks to my two sons, Grant and Ben, who give me joy every day. We are the lucky ones to have you in our family.

To my good friends who served as advance readers – Heather Sisan, Jamie Bellis, Anne Baum – I appreciate you so much, and I owe you one.

I primarily wrote this book so that adopted children and mixed-race children could see themselves reflected in this story. It's my small contribution to the broader effort to not stay silent in the face of injustice, racism and prejudice.

CHAPTER

ONE

I THREW A PERFECT-SIZED stick as far as I could. It sailed all the way across our yard, and my foster dog Willow took off like a furry bullet. She's faster than anything I've ever seen. She almost caught the stick before it landed near a tall tree that was swaying back and forth fiercely, thanks to the wind.

Willow is a yellow Lab puppy. I love her more than anything in the world. Well, maybe I love lacrosse more. But Willow is at least tied with lacrosse.

I kept throwing the stick for Willow for a long time. It's her favorite game. She tossed the stick to herself and caught it again. She's a smart dog. It made me happy to see her so happy, wagging her tail and shaking her stick.

Willow came from an organization that trains puppies that will grow up to become service dogs for veterans. We found out this group needed families to take care of the puppies for their first 18 months, since they can't do service training when they're too young. The hard part is they have to leave you when they're old enough to go to training and help a veteran.

My brother, Matt, and I begged and begged our mom and dad to get a dog, and eventually they agreed. "But Carter," Mom said, "you have to promise to help walk her, even if it's raining or snowing all day long. You're old enough for it now that you're 11. Matt, you can feed her."

I don't know why parents make up dumb promises like that, but they do it pretty often. "Okay, Mom, I'll do it!" What else could I say at that point?

We picked up Willow back in January, when she was ready to leave her mother at around eight weeks old. She was so tiny then, barely bigger than my hands. Now she's 10 months old.

I saw an old tennis ball under one of our bushes, so I picked it up and threw it for Willow. She ran at top speed and caught it before it hit the ground.

"Good girl!" I cheered.

She gave the ball to me, and I threw it again and again. I was careful to make sure Willow stayed away from the thorny bush in the far end of the yard. She looked really big to me as she ran across our back yard. She keeps growing more and more. Her ears are so soft, it's like touching cotton candy, except not sticky.

Our most important job is to keep her healthy and socialize her, so she gets along very well with people and other dogs. We also taught her basic obedience, like how to walk on a leash, sit and stay, and come when we call her name. It's fun to teach her things.

To train future service dogs, you need to take them to all kinds of places like restaurants, church, school, lacrosse practices, the library, and the dog park. You even take them on boring errands like grocery shopping and picking up the dry cleaning.

When we go out in public, Willow wears a little blue vest that says she's a future service dog. It's really cool to think that one day she will be able to help somebody open doors, pick up things off the floor, carry bags, get undressed, or get out of bed.

"Carter!" Mom called in a sing-song way. "Dinner's ready! Bring Willow inside."

CHAPTER
TWO

AFTER DINNER, THE doorbell rang. John and Jalen wanted to hang out. The three of us have been best friends forever. We used to play trains and Legos and hide-and-seek together in preschool. It was in one wing of a church building with a big red door. When we got older, we played kickball and football together every day at recess. We live in a big suburb in Maryland with tons of trees and parks and bike paths, where I walk Willow after school.

It was a mild evening in early September. The three of us raced our bikes around our neighborhood, trading jokes and insults. At first, Willow tried to follow me, but I told her, "Not this time, girl." The air felt a little chilly. It was starting to get darker outside. We paused when we got to John's house.

John's two older brothers were casually tossing a football around in their front yard, which was partially covered in crunchy leaves. They are superstar football players at their high school. Not just pretty good, but so great that cheerleaders and even some adults act like they have a celebrity crush. For John, growing up with them, it was clearly going to be too hard to live up to their huge talent on the football field, so John favored lacrosse instead. He's been obsessed with it ever since second grade.

"You want to study for the math test?" Jalen asked John.

"Sure," said John. They're both in advanced math, and I'm in regular math. They help me with my math homework sometimes.

"Carter, can you help me revise my essay later, if you're not too busy preparing for the National Spelling Bee?" John asked me. English is by far my best subject. I won one spelling bee in the third grade, and John never lets me forget it.

"Sure, Skinny Ankles. See you guys later!"

Jalen gave me a fist bump. He's a huge gamer. He plays Madden 20 and Mario Kart all the time. He teaches me how to drift like a gaming beast. He loves comic books, too, and he knows everything about every Marvel movie ever made. He's the kind of friend who stands up for you and doesn't talk bad about people behind their backs. He would never roast anyone on social media.

John is white, and Jalen is black, like me. Most of the time, that stuff never mattered too much to us. But I'm starting to see things changing. We don't have class all day long together like we used to in elementary school, but we eat lunch together now when we can. In the cafeteria, I always see the Korean kids eating together and the black kids eating together and the white kids eating together. I don't like it. It wasn't that way in elementary school.

I watched as the two of them stepped into John's house, one with short brown hair and the other with black cornrows. Years of friendship made them walk with an easy familiarity and unity. I felt lucky to share that same thing with both of them.

CHAPTER

THREE

WHEN I WAS little, I didn't know I was black. I just knew I looked like me. That's all I've ever known. It's obvious I was adopted because my parents are white. Skin color didn't seem like something that mattered at all until I was about five or six.

When I was in kindergarten, a girl on the playground asked why my mom didn't look like me. My mom told her about how I was adopted. The girl was satisfied with the answer, even though she was still a little confused. I didn't mind the question at all. I'm used to looking different from Mom and Dad, since I've lived with them my whole life.

After a while, I started to realize that being black wasn't the same as being white because of history. In second grade, I read books about black people trying to escape slavery. There's a book about a guy who mailed himself to Philadelphia inside a box. That really happened.

It still wasn't great for black people, even long after slavery ended. I read about the Green Book, which somebody wrote to help black people know the safe places to stop when they were traveling. White people wouldn't let black people stay in certain hotels or eat in certain restaurants, even when they had money to pay for it.

It sounded awful and painful. If we lived back then, I wouldn't be allowed to go to school with John because of my skin color. That's something I try not to think about.

Sometimes I hear white people try to be nice and say things like "race doesn't matter" or "we don't see color." That's so annoying because it's a total lie. Maybe it feels like race doesn't matter if you're in the majority, but it matters a lot when you're in the oppressed group.

I used to feel kind of special to be adopted and brown-skinned. I'm not so sure about that now. Sometimes being adopted makes me feel weird or embarrassed. It depends, but a lot of days, it's no fun being different. In my sixth grade class, there's a couple of other kids who are adopted, too. But it's not like we sit around talking about it all the time.

Some of those kids actually look like their adopted parents, but not me. I don't get the option of choosing who knows about my adoption (unless I hide my parents, of course, but that's not a real option when you can't drive yourself anywhere).

Mom and Dad met my birth mom, Imani, at the hospital in Maryland when I was born. We have three photos of her from that day. In one photo, she is cradling me on her left shoulder and rubbing my back with her right hand. She's wearing light blue jeans and a red T-shirt with the Old Bay logo.

I've always wondered if she likes crabs and Old Bay. Everyone says it's a Maryland thing. Maybe Imani's fingertips smell like Old Bay, like mine do when I eat crabs. I would like that. Mom says I'm obsessed with food, but I say so what? Food connects people, just like music does.

The other two photos are close ups of Imani's face, looking at me tenderly.

Other than that first day, we haven't heard from my birth mom. No emails or texts or phone calls. Mom and Dad send letters and photos of me every year to the adoption agency, so she can get those if she wants to. We don't know if she has read them or not.

My birth father is her ex-boyfriend, and he moved away before I was born. We don't know where he is. I've never seen a picture of him. Not even once.

In my mind, he looks like John Cena. I imagine he's an Air Force pilot, flying cargo all over the world, wearing a camouflage uniform. It makes me think of speed and power and the smell of pure, fresh air.

My birth mom is black, and my birth father is white. My skin is light golden brown, and it gets slightly darker in the summer.

One more weird fact: My feet are so wide that Dad stopped trying to buy me sneakers at Kohls and Target years ago. Instead, he has to order super-wide ones for me online. I wonder if my wide feet come from my birth mom's side or my birth dad's side.

Going back to adoption, it's basically the same story for my brother, Matt, and his birthparents. No contact so far, but maybe it's possible in the future. Matt's birth parents are both black. His skin is medium brown, a few shades darker than mine.

He's in third grade, three years younger than me. He can be annoying, like when he hogs the couch and smells up the bathroom right when I need it. I don't like it when he brings home good report cards and brags all about it, as if he's the only kid in the history of Maryland who got A's on a report card. My grades are fine, but not quite as good as his.

Mom and Dad are both freckle-faced and blue-eyed. His heritage is German, and hers is Dutch and Irish. On a genealogy website, they were able to look up when their ancestors sailed to the United States and passed through Ellis Island. They know when their parents came to Maryland.

Unlike them, sometimes I feel like my life will always have a lot of unanswered questions. Will I ever meet my birth parents? How tall is my birth father? Does my birth mom's voice sound rough and raspy like my art teacher's? There's a lot I don't know. Maybe I just have to live with that, but it's hard.

Then there's the Big Question: Why didn't my birth parents take care of me? Was something wrong with me? Maybe I cried too much in the hospital. Or maybe I was defective and unlovable. It's as if Mom and Dad got stuck with the package that nobody else wanted.

Mom and Dad said my birth parents couldn't take care of me because they didn't have enough money. But couldn't one of them borrow some money from a relative or something? I don't understand it at all. Was my birth mom sad when she left me? Does she think about me sometimes? I don't know.

One thing my birth parents don't know is how much I love lacrosse. I feel strong and fearless on the field. Lacrosse gives me extra confidence that I don't usually have off the field. I wonder if my athletic skills come from my birth mom's side or my birth dad's side.

I love how lacrosse is a fast-moving game with a lot of quick thinking and running. I love being outdoors for the all the practices and games. Baseball and basketball are nothing like lacrosse. Soccer is a bit closer, but still not the same.

Anyway, my team is the Ellicott Mills Eagles. It's a travel team that trains almost year-round and plays in several tournaments every year. Coach Sam pushes us hard to get better, but he also wants us to have fun. He's fair with playing time, and he helps us work together as a team. We're better together than we ever could be individually.

CHAPTER

FOUR

MOM PICKED ME up at school early and took me to the dentist, Dr. Jenkins. I hate going to the dentist. The chemical smell of it, the sound of the machines, the holding my mouth open at uncomfortable angles for such a long time. I'd rather be doing anything else.

We waited for about 10 minutes. Then the blonde lady behind the desk called, "Carter Young?" Mom and I stood up and walked up to the desk.

"Are you his mother?"

"Yes, I am," said Mom. I could see she was tensing up in her shoulders a little bit.

The blonde lady raised her eyebrows, as if she wasn't sure she should believe what she was hearing.

"Can I see your driver's license?"

"I'm his mother," Mom said. She sewed her lips together in a straight line. She reached inside her purse to get her wallet to show her ID.

"Unless you are the parent, you can't go back to the treatment room with him," the lady said flatly.

Mom handed over her ID, and the lady looked at it briefly and opened the door for us to come through. Walking along the hallway to the treatment room, Mom's steps were louder and faster than normal. Her jaw was set.

"Mom, don't worry about it," I said. I wanted to shrink and disappear immediately. I did not want to be there anymore. How long would this appointment take?

After the dentist arrived, everything went fine. Mom relaxed a bit. The dentist was pretty easy-going and gentle during the exam. It still hurt a little. Lucky for me, no cavities.

When we got home, Dad was in the middle of making a salad for dinner. He asked how the dentist appointment was.

"That office administrator was really rude," Mom said. "She looked at me like she didn't believe I was Carter's mother."

"What happened?" Dad asked.

"She wanted to see my driver's license, so I gave it to her. Do you think she asks all the other parents for their IDs? Probably not."

"Sounds like she let a little power go to her head."

"Around here, she shouldn't be so surprised to see an adopted kid. There's plenty of kids in their school who are adopted. There's Abby, Ava, Jasmine, John Cutter, Eddie Smith."

Mom was on a roll. She was getting worked up again. Dad gave her a shoulder rub, and she relaxed her whole posture. She started chopping some celery for the salad. Willow licked Mom's ankles, which made Mom smile. I loved how Willow was so good at cheering us up when we're upset.

CHAPTER

FIVE

IT WAS OUR second lacrosse game of the season, against a team from Pasadena. They were playing rougher than most teams we'd seen before, but I wasn't worried about it. There were a few clouds over the field, but no rain so far.

At halftime, we were up 5 to 4. I was quick enough to intercept a pass and send the ball to my teammate, Chris. He took it up the field and made a shot, which came close, but didn't go into the goal.

A minute later, I intercepted another pass and gave it to my best friend John, who was open. The other team's defender almost got it away from him, but John managed to advance toward the goal and pass it to Chris, who took a shot and scored. I heard the parents clapping.

The other team's midfielder hovered next to me, looking super-angry and frustrated. He muttered, "Why don't you go play basketball? Go put your basketball shoes on." His jersey said he was #10.

I was stunned. I just kept concentrating on the ball and getting open for my teammates. I'm a midfielder because I'm fast and good at passing. I knew #10 was harassing me because of my skin color. I'm the only black kid on my team. Most of the time, I'm the only black kid on the field. I was pissed, and I started exhaling hard through my nose. I was ready to demolish that Pasadena team.

"Eyes up, Carter!" Coach Sam called. "Bring it up the field!"

I caught an incoming pass, but I only had the ball for a second before #8 hit my arm with his stick, and the ball flew out of the net. The ref called slashing. Then #8 turned to me and said bitterly, "So what? I'm still better than you, monkey boy." He glared at me and shot a smug look at #10.

John must have heard what he said because John suddenly looked furious, like his head was about to explode. I didn't want to let my opponent get into my head. I tried to stay calm, but my insides were madder than ever. My teeth clenched together, and my shoulders tightened.

"Keep cool, boys!" Coach Sam called. "You've got this!"

A minute later, right after #10 made a pass, John aggressively body checked him, and the ref called illegal body checking. In that moment, #10 looked like he was so ready to fight.

I ran up the field to try to take the ball away from the midfielder, who had grabbed it. I almost got it, but I fell hard on my knee when #10 tripped me. Somehow, the ref missed it. I could hear Coach Sam calling loudly, "Tripping!"

A few guys started making monkey sounds. Then #10 laughed harshly and said, "What's the matter? Can't stay on your feet, monkey boy?" More monkey sounds and laughing.

Without thinking, I shoved him. John tackled him to the ground. Some guys on the other team started grabbing and punching me and John. Everything was happening so fast. Somewhere in all the chaos, another guy's elbow struck my cheekbone hard. The pain in my head was almost blinding. I held my face in my two hands.

At some point, the coaches ran onto the field to stop the fight. Everyone was yelling so loud: players, coaches, parents, kids. It was hard to make sense of it all. John and I told the ref what the other guys said. John's face was redder than I had ever seen it. Even his ears were red. The ref threw me, John, #10 and #8 out of the game.

I hated that team from Pasadena. The pit of my belly felt hot with exertion, adrenaline and fury. I wanted to pummel a punching bag until my hands hurt. I wanted to run until my lungs burst. Instead, John and I had to sit on the bench, wishing we could get back into the game to crush the other team. Sitting still was killing me. I looked at Mom and Dad to see if there were any signs that they understood everything that had happened. They were watching the game intently.

Nobody played well after the fight. We ended up winning 9-8. But I didn't feel victorious or upbeat at all. Suddenly, the win hardly mattered to me. My cheek hurt, and I was not sure I wanted to play lacrosse anymore.

Did people really think I looked like an ape? Maybe I am kind of ugly. Mom doesn't think so, but maybe she's just being nice because she's my mom. These thoughts were making my head hurt more.

After the game ended, some of the parents from both teams started yelling at each other. Everyone else was staring, wondering what would come next.

John's dad yelled, "They have no right to talk like that! It's racist! What are you teaching your kids?"

A tall white man screamed, "He can say what he wants! If you ridiculous ninnies don't like it, leave! Go back to your suburban snowflake hellhole!"

The place went silent, totally stunned. It was scary. With Dad and Matt close behind us, Mom steered me away from the crowd, walking us toward our car. She put her arm around me and said quietly, "Carter, are you okay? That looks like it's going to be a pretty big bruise on your face."

"I'm okay," I said. "Those guys were stupid racists."

"I know, honey. I know. I'm sorry they said those awful things. It was very wrong what they did," Mom said. She gave me a huge hug and took a closer look at my cheek, which was starting to swell more. Mom smelled like lavender, like she always does. That made me feel safe. "Let's go home."

Leaving the field, Matt was so mad he wanted to beat up those punks single-handedly. He kept looking back at them with a glare so fierce you'd never think it could have come out of an eight-year-old.

"Thanks, bro," I said softly.

I do sort of love my brother, although a lot of days I'm too annoyed at him to admit it.

Back at home, I put an ice pack on my cheek and watched the Ravens game on the couch with Matt. I didn't feel like doing anything else. I was so deeply tired from head to toe. Willow jumped onto the couch and curled into my lap. She felt so warm and cozy. I tried to forget about the pain for a while.

CHAPTER

SIX

THE NEXT DAY, Uncle Brian and Aunt Laura came over for dinner. They live about 20 minutes from our house. Mom told them what happened at the lacrosse game.

"I'm going to figure out how I can file a complaint with the league. What happened to Carter was really racist," she said.

Uncle Brian said, "Don't worry about it. They're just talking trash. It doesn't mean anything."

Mom said, "No, it's not right."

Uncle Brian laughed it off. "You didn't play sports with boys. They talk trash all the time. You just have to ignore it."

Mom's eyes got tighter, and the crease between her eyes got deeper. "No, this is different. It's unacceptable." She was starting to get her courtroom look. It's something I've seen before when she needs to win a big case. She's a lawyer for the state Department of Aging. She doesn't back down from a fight against injustice.

Uncle Brian shook his head. His reddish brown beard looked shorter than usual. "Look," he said, "Boys will be boys. Don't make a big fuss over it and bring race into it when you don't need to. That makes it worse."

Mom passed around a platter of chicken enchiladas, which Matt likes, and I don't. I think they're too spicy.

I saw Uncle Brian give Aunt Laura a look that seemed to suggest "see, what did I tell you?" I was getting super-uncomfortable. I felt like Mom was probably right, but I was still confused. Uncle Brian's usually a good guy. He takes me to Star Wars movies, and we have a lot of fun. He's a huge sports fan and watches football and soccer with us sometimes. Why didn't he see how bad those Pasadena guys were?

There was an awkward silence. Matt's eyes were shooting arrows at Uncle Brian. Dad started talking about the Ravens game against the Steelers. That sort of broke the ice and got us back into our normal rhythm for a while. I passed the sour cream to Aunt Laura.

After dinner, I didn't want to stay in the kitchen with Uncle Brian. I went up to my room to play Fortnite, but it didn't make me feel any better. I just couldn't get my head in the game. I gave up after a while.

Dad came up to my room and nudged the door halfway open. "Want to talk for a bit?" he asked.

"Okay."

"Yesterday's game was pretty stressful. Are you feeling okay?"

"I guess so. Just mad at those guys on the other team. And Uncle Brian didn't get it at all."

"Yeah, Carter, it's true that sometimes people, even people you love, won't understand what you're going through when you're dealing with racism. It doesn't mean Uncle Brian doesn't love you. It just means he hasn't experienced the same things himself, so he's not so great at understanding it."

"Okay. But why did he take their side? I'm his nephew."

"That's right. You are. Maybe Uncle Brian needs some more time to see things from your perspective," Dad said. "Just know your mom and I are always on your side. Any time you experience something like what happened at the game, we're there for you."

"I know."

"Those things they said about you – you know they're not true, right?" Dad said. "Just because people said terrible things about you doesn't make it true. You know who you are. You are loved and valued as a person just as much as anybody else. And you belong on that field just as much as anybody else."

I gave Dad a hug. I breathed a little deeper, relaxing my shoulders.

"Does it bother you, playing in a mostly white sport?" Dad asked.

"I don't know. It didn't used to, but maybe it does now."

"You're really good at lacrosse, Carter. If you really love it, stay with it. Just realize that sometimes you might face some difficult situations and ignorant people. That could happen in any sport or any group."

"That doesn't sound very encouraging."

"What I mean is, you should do what you love, and don't let them hold you back from doing it. You're brave, Carter."

"Okay. Thanks, Dad."

When I thought about going back to the same lacrosse field for another game, I felt really uncomfortable and uneasy. My stomach started to clench. But I also didn't like the idea of quitting lacrosse, either. I've worked so hard at it. I'd miss out on so much if I wasn't a part of the team anymore. Could I even imagine sitting at home while everyone else was competing in games and tournaments together? I felt stuck.

Uncle Brian had it easy when he was a kid. He never had to deal with stuff like this when he played baseball in middle and high school. He has no clue what it's like. Me and Matt, we both have some extra weight to carry all the time, along with all the typical human baggage.

I picked up my math homework and finished the rest of it. My decision about lacrosse could wait for another day.

Drake's song pulsed in my headphones.

> *I been movin' calm. Don't start no trouble with me.*
> *Tryna keep it peaceful is a struggle for me.*

I let the music drown out all the rest of my thoughts. Drake is mixed like me. It's rare for me to see somebody who's mixed. My town is pretty diverse, but I just don't see that that many mixed kids. Maybe that will change in the future.

CHAPTER

SEVEN

A T SCHOOL ON Monday, lots of guys were talking about what happened at the lacrosse game. They were texting each other about it constantly, too, even though they weren't supposed to be texting during school. In the hallways and the cafeteria, they kept asking me random questions about it. I really didn't want all that attention. I tried to explain it as quickly as possible, so I could move on.

John gave me a fist bump when we passed each other in the hall. He's a real friend. A friend forever.

In English class, Mr. Harvey gave us our next assignment: Read a biography of a historical figure and write a book report about it. At the end of class, he pulled me aside and said, "Got any ideas of who you might like to do your book report on?"

"No, not really," I said.

"So I hear you're pretty good at lacrosse. You might consider a book on Jim Brown. Do you know who he is?"

"No."

"He was the first black lacrosse legend," Mr. Harvey explained.

"Really?"

"Yeah. Just some food for thought. You can choose someone else if you want."

"Thanks, Mr. Harvey."

He's a pretty cool teacher. A huge Ravens fan, too. I wondered if he overheard kids talking about our lacrosse game.

After lunch, I looked up Jim Brown on Wikipedia at the school library. He was one of the best players in NFL history. He was an incredible running back for the Cleveland Browns in the 1960s. He grew up in Long Island and played midfield for Syracuse University's lacrosse team. He was inducted into the Pro Football Hall of Fame and the Lacrosse Hall of Fame.

I found a book on him in the biography section. The more I read about him, the more impressed I was. His middie skills were unstoppable. Why had I never heard about him before? It just proves those guys from Pasadena were wrong all along, even more than they realized. Lacrosse does not belong to white people. Shouldn't that be obvious to everyone? Lacrosse started out as a Native American game. How did it turn into a white sport?

Seeing Jim Brown's picture, I felt angry and proud at the same time. That doesn't make sense, but it's the truth. I was proud to clearly see in writing that someone like me belongs in lacrosse just as much as anyone else. But I was also angry at having no control over racism that blindsides me. It's a totally helpless feeling, like being handcuffed in a fight against a heavyweight champion.

Jim Brown got me thinking more about staying on the lacrosse team. If he could do it, I could do it, right? At least, I wanted to try. That's when I decided to keep playing lacrosse, at least for this season.

I put two books on Jim Brown in my backpack to read later. I was curious to learn more. Mr. Harvey was right about this one.

Mom decided not to bring a complaint to the lacrosse league, but she did write a no-nonsense letter to the editor of the local newspaper, which published it quickly. I was proud of her for that.

A few of the other moms from the lacrosse team suggested the idea of wearing black and white wristbands to all the games. They were soccer fans who remembered a Manchester United player who designed wristbands to protest racism. In less than a week, these determined moms passed out about five dozen wristbands to lacrosse players, family members and friends. I never knew something like this would mean so much to them. I wore my wristband everywhere, and so did Matt and John.

CHAPTER

EIGHT

AT OUR NEXT practice on Tuesday, Coach Sam talked to all of us about sportsmanship and what actions can get us penalized or removed from a game. He talked about how wrong racism is, no matter where it happens, including the lacrosse field or the basketball court or the hockey rink.

"Heated competition does not justify using racist language. Everyone who did that on Saturday was wrong," Coach Sam said. "But I also want you to think carefully about how you respond to insults and racist remarks. Should you punch the other guy in the face? Does it help anyone if you get yourself expelled from the game by pushing or punching your opponents? I've always taught you guys that it never pays to play dirty. Keep your playing clean, and keep your temper in check. I know it's hard to do that in the heat of the game. I won't tolerate racism, so you can come to me anytime a player is using racist language, whether he's from our team or another team. Everybody understand?"

Lots of heads nodded yes. It seemed like everyone got it.

I felt good as we went through our drills and played a short scrimmage. It was a relief to put my mind completely on lacrosse and not think about anything else. I ran at full speed and felt a satisfying burn in my lungs. At the end of practice, I felt really tired in a good way. I chugged the rest of my water and slowly walked over to the parking lot.

I could hear my teammate, Chris, talking to his dad, but they couldn't see me, since they were on the other side of a row of cars. "Coach gave us some lame speech about racism and stuff. Such a waste of time when we could have been practicing," Chris complained.

"Yeah, well, it's all about being politically correct these days," his dad replied in a dismissive tone. "Just stupidity. There's no racism in lacrosse. That's in the past."

I was frozen for a minute. Did they really think those hurtful things? I never knew. I didn't think they would say stuff like that in front of me. It made me wonder how many other guys on my team thought the same thing, even after what happened at our game.

Chris was never my close friend, but we've always been sort of friendly. Maybe it was fake all along. I felt like I saw Chris's real self in those few moments in the parking lot. I hate fake people.

I didn't say anything to Mom about it during the car ride home, but I kept turning it over in my mind. At home on the couch, Willow curled up on my lap, and I stroked her ears and neck, which she likes a lot. Is it wrong to trust white people like Chris? Do I need to be more guarded all the time? That sounded exhausting.

I wished I could talk to my birth father. I bet he would understand this better than my parents do. Some days, I kind of want to talk with Mom and Dad about my feelings. Other times, I'd rather spend an hour picking up dog poop than talk about how I'm feeling, especially about things like race and adoption. It's easier to try to not think about it. Easier to keep it inside. At least in the moment, it felt that way.

That's the great thing about dogs like Willow. They understand how you're feeling without any words. How do they do that?

CHAPTER

NINE

JOHN AND JALEN were both absent when I walked into the middle school cafeteria on Wednesday. John had the flu, and Jalen had a dentist appointment. I paused briefly and looked around for someone to sit with.

Two black kids, Demarcus and Elijah, sat in the back corner, and I steered myself toward them. I've been friends with them since second or third grade. Demarcus makes us laugh with all his crazy jokes, and he has some halfway decent dance moves, which is definitely more than I can say for myself. I can't even floss.

Elijah is quiet in class and probably the best basketball player in our class. He almost never misses a shot. For a second, I felt a bit of nervousness, since I don't usually eat lunch with them. But I kept going anyway.

For the next five minutes, they were talking nonstop about their favorite basketball team, the Lakers. Sometimes people think I should know everything about basketball because I'm black. It's kind of annoying. The truth is, I don't know much about basketball, and I don't really like it. Demarcus and Elijah could see I wasn't completely following their fast banter.

"Look at Carter. He don't know who Anthony Davis is!" Elijah said. "You too white, man!" He gave a genuine smile and landed a light punch on my shoulder to let me know it was just a little friendly joking. I laughed and traded an insult back to him.

Demarcus started talking about how the school French fries were disgusting and how he can't wait for his grandma to make his favorite sweet potato pie on Sunday. He went on and on about it like he could taste it just by thinking about it.

"Yeah, sweet potato pie is amazing. It crushes pumpkin," I agreed.

"That's what I'm talkin' 'bout!" said Elijah.

I look forward to my mom's sweet potato pie at Thanksgiving every year. She makes it because she knows I like it. My mom is a really good cook when she's not making enchiladas. For some reason, Dad prefers pumpkin pie. That's what his mom used to make every year.

I noticed how Elijah and Demarcus bought lunch in the cafeteria almost every day, but I always brought a lame bologna sandwich from home. They guzzled down Sprite, and I drank water. Maybe that stuff doesn't really matter. I wasn't sure. I still felt a little awkward with them, like maybe I could never fit in because I'm not black enough. But I'm not white enough, either.

I remembered how last month someone wrote on the bathroom wall "RDS is an Oreo." Everyone knew it meant Raymond DeSantis, a mixed kid in seventh grade. Oreo means black on the outside and white on the inside.

I don't know if Raymond ever saw it. I heard the janitor cleaned it up pretty fast, but I don't know if anyone got in trouble for it. Did people say the same thing about me? What about Bruno Mars?

Did anyone call him an Oreo when he was in middle school? That's crazy talk.

It's weird, but sometimes I find myself changing my words and my voice to sound more like Demarcus and Elijah when I'm around them. I don't even mean to do it. It just kind of happens. I guess it shows I want to fit in with the kids at school. But it also feels like survival.

Being an Oreo means you don't belong anywhere. It means you get attacked from both sides. I wondered if it's fake when I sound like the black kids. I don't want to be fake. Not ever. Being fake is the worst. But being different is pretty bad, too. It's worse when the different part of you is something that you can't change about yourself, something you have no control over.

CHAPTER

TEN

I T WAS TERRIFYING as we drove to my next lacrosse game on Saturday. What would these opponents be like? Would there be another brawl? I almost wanted to tell Dad to turn the car around. But I'm glad I didn't. Once we got in our familiar places, executing our familiar plays, it felt right and normal to me. I could tell my endurance was increasing. We lost by one point, but overall we played really well.

On Sunday, the sun was bright, but the air was chilly as I walked outside to get the mail. It was just a few advertising fliers and one postcard that said NEWARK in big block letters with some buildings in the design. It was from Imani Jones. My birth mom!

It said, "Hi from Newark. Text me sometime. XO, Imani Jones" with her phone number scrawled underneath.

The news hit me with such a forceful shock that I sat down right there on the curb next to the mailbox. I didn't move, not even an eyelash, for what seemed like 10 minutes. I felt confused and excited and amazed, all at the same time. It would mean so much to talk with her, even for a few minutes.

Finally, I stood up and took the mail inside, sliding the postcard into my backpack. My breathing was faster than normal. My heart pounded hard on my chest bone. I had so many questions. Does she live in New Jersey now? Does she look older? Does she have other kids? They would be my half-siblings, I guess.

I didn't know how to bring it up to Mom and Dad. It felt strange or awkward somehow. I knew I shouldn't hide it from them, but I couldn't figure out how to talk about it. Family is so complicated.

We went to Matt's soccer game, and I didn't say anything about the postcard. Later we ate dinner. Spaghetti and meatballs, which I barely nibbled. That was strange because I normally take a second helping of my mom's delicious spaghetti and meatballs. I kept thinking about the postcard, but when I tried to say something about it, I just couldn't find the words.

At bedtime, Mom came into my room to say goodnight, giving me a quick kiss on the forehead.

"Mom, can I go to Newark?"

"What? You mean Newark, New Jersey? Why do you want to go there, honey?" Mom asked in a puzzled voice.

"I think my birth mom is there. Can we go to see her?"

"Your birth mom? What makes you think she's there?"

"I got a postcard from her."

"You did? A postcard from New Jersey?" Mom said, still dumbfounded. "Can I see it?"

"I really want to go. Can we go see her?"

"I don't think so. Newark's a pretty far way to go. Maybe when you're older."

I felt my head getting tighter, almost as if my brain was expanding. I felt a surge of rage, surprisingly fast. I wanted to hit something.

"It's not that far! You don't care, do you? You don't get it at all!" I screamed. I turned away from Mom, wrapping both my arms around my chest.

"Don't get what?" Her blue eyes were big when I glanced a at her again.

"Shut up! I don't want to talk to you!" I screamed. "Go away!" I threw a random book at the nearest wall.

Mom took a few steps back. Her eyes were darkened and furious. "No way are you going to New Jersey!" she yelled. "Not when you talk to your mother like that!" Her voice sounded shocked.

She left quickly with loud foot stomps traveling down the stairs. I stared at the spot where she had been standing, now empty. I laid on my bed, listening to music, for a long time. *This is so unfair. Will I ever get to meet my birth parents?*

Then Mom knocked on the door gently. "Honey, I'm sorry," she said. Her eyes were soft.

"I'm sorry for throwing the book."

"I know. I shouldn't have said you can't go to Newark. What I meant was Dad and I want to get to know your birth mom more before you can have phone calls and visits with her. We just want to keep you safe."

"I am safe."

"We don't know anything about what your birth mom is like and what's going on in her life right now. We need more information, Carter."

"She's not an axe murderer."

"I know, honey. Maybe we can all visit her after we understand some things a little better."

I sighed and closed my eyes. I didn't want to wait. I had already waited long enough. But I do love my Mom and Dad, even when I'm mad at them.

"How long?"

"I don't know," she said. "It depends."

I turned away from her, hardening my jaw. *She won't understand. She doesn't care about any of this. It's not fair.*

"Can I see the postcard?" Mom asked.

I closed my eyes and pretended to sleep. Mom patted me on the leg, as if that was the end of that. I was tired, but I couldn't fall asleep for a long time. Willow hopped onto my bed and rested on top of my feet. Her weight on my feet felt comforting. Then she licked my leg, which tickled and almost made me giggle for a second until I remembered how mad I was.

I looked at my birth mom's photos. Would I even recognize her now if I saw her pass by on the street? In the photos, her hair is dark and curly, brushing her shoulders. Her nose is large and broad. Her mouth looks like mine.

It felt weird to know that I grew inside her, but I don't know her. Not really. And she doesn't know me. She never saw me play lacrosse or learn to read or ride a bike. She doesn't know about the time I got stiches in the back of my head because I leaned too far back in a plastic chair and fell on our cement patio two years ago. Or that time I puked on the Metro on the way home from the Cherry Blossom Festival. Or the fact that I dressed up as Dumbledore for Halloween two years in a row.

I stared and stared at the photos, as if that could make me remember what it was like to be with her. I felt like there was something missing, some memory that was fighting to come through. Was there a clue in one of the photos, something I hadn't noticed before? If I could remember being a baby, that would take away the missing feeling.

I shook my head, trying to make the confusion go away. It didn't work. With one arm around Willow, I shut my eyes tight, still mad at Mom. After a while, I fell into a sleep that wasn't very restful.

CHAPTER

ELEVEN

ON MONDAY, MY mind was still brewing over the fight with Mom. I wrote Imani's number on a piece of paper and tucked it into my backpack. Then I casually gave the postcard to Mom as I left for school. I didn't forgive her, but I figured I wasn't doing myself any good by keeping the postcard to myself.

During lunch, I asked John if I could use his phone to make a call. I don't have a cellphone. My parents said I'm too young. It's so stupid. How am I too young if all the kids my age have one? It doesn't make any sense.

After I found a hallway corner with a little privacy, I stared at John's phone, almost too afraid to press the buttons. What would Imani think of me? Would she think I was too babyish because I didn't have my own cellphone? I hit the numbers and listened to the ringing. My breath got faster.

"Hello?"

"Hi? This is Carter."

"Oh my god, Carter! So you got my postcard," she said, sounding pleased.

"Yeah." I liked Imani's voice. It's gentle and soft, kind of like Zendaya's voice.

"How you doin'?" she asked.

"I'm okay."

"You at school?" she asked.

"Yeah."

"I don't wanna keep you from your classes."

"It's okay. Did you get the letters and photos we sent to the agency?"

"No. I didn't do that yet." She sounded regretful. "The adoption agency gave me your address."

"Thanks for the postcard."

"Oh, no problem," she laughed. It was kind, full-belly laugh. It sounded wonderful.

"It's good to hear your voice, Carter," she said.

"Yeah, you, too."

"So you have a brother or sister?"

"Yeah. Matt. He's 9."

"He adopted, too?

"Yeah."

There was a long pause. I didn't know what to say. Maybe she didn't, either.

"Do you have kids? I mean, besides me."

"Yeah, my baby girl is 5."

"Oh, wow," I said. Suddenly, I felt like I had a million more questions to ask her. I wanted time to stop, so I wouldn't have to go back to class.

"What's her name?"

"Rayna," she said.

Part of me was really, truly happy to have a half-sister. Part of me was fiercely jealous. Why did she keep Rayna and not me? The money excuse must be a lie, if she can take care of Rayna. It made no sense to me. I felt a pain in my upper belly.

"She's in kindergarten. On the way to school, we love to sing the Frozen songs in the car," Imani said.

That's one thing we don't have in common. My singing voice is barely mediocre. Not like Demarcus. He can really sing like Bruno Mars.

There was more phone silence. Talking on the phone with my birth mom wasn't as easy as I thought it would be. I wondered if it would be better in person. The school bell rang.

"I better get to English class," I said.

"Okay. Call me again sometime if you want," Imani said.

"Okay. I will."

I inhaled some huge breaths. I didn't even realize I was holding my breath during the call. I thought I would feel super joyful if I got to talk to my birth mom, but I actually felt nervous and sad and happy, all at the same time.

She seemed nice. Talking to her made me sad that I can't see her. Also sad about all the time I didn't spend with her for the last 11 years. I missed her a lot. How would my life have been different with her? I don't know. It's hard to imagine not being with Mom and Dad and Matt.

I wondered why my birth mom didn't get in touch before now. And what made her decide to send a postcard now?

I gave John's phone back to him and walked with him to English class. My brain just didn't want to focus on things like symbolism and textual evidence in "A Wrinkle In Time."

I kept replaying the phone call in my head. What would it have been like if she had kept me? Would I still be the way I am now?

When I got home later, Willow ran to greet me and nuzzled her head into my palm. I rubbed behind her ear and gave her a bacon-flavored treat, which she finished off in less than one second.

"How was school?" Mom asked.

"Pretty good," I said. "Mom, don't get mad at me about this, but … during lunch I talked to my birth mom."

There was a very long pause. Mom's face looked a little surprised, but not mad. Like maybe she knew this day was coming.

"Oh, you did? What did she say?"

"Well, I have a half-sister called Rayna."

"Oh, wow," Mom said with her eyebrows raised.

"She's 5."

Mom smiled. A real, genuine smile. "What do you think about that?"

"Pretty cool," I said, looking at the trees outside the kitchen window.

"Are you curious to learn more about your birth mom?"

"Yeah," I said quietly.

"Well, the postcard could be a start to build a relationship," Mom said. "Let's see how it goes. Try not to build up huge expectations yet. Just take it day by day. Sound fair?"

"Yeah, okay."

"I know your birth mom and your half-sister are a part of you, and I don't want to take that away from you."

I nodded. Mom gave me one of her extra big hugs that smelled like lavender. That's when I forgave her.

CHAPTER

TWELVE

O N SATURDAY, MATT and I watched "Hotel for Dogs" for the third time. We still love it. Never gets old. After the movie stopped, the Roku started automatically showing some family photos.

"Look at how bad your volleyball skills were," Matt teased me, tilting his chin toward a photo of us three years ago, with me swinging wildly at a volleyball in Ocean City. I laughed and teased, "Well, look at your SpongeBob bathing suit. So uncool!" He laughed and tossed some popcorn at me.

The next photo was another beach shot with me and Dad, his arm around me, standing near the waves. This one was from last summer. Something left an unpleasant taste in my mouth, like eating tuna salad with a metallic twinge. I realized what it was. Next to Dad, my brown skin stood out too much. Like maybe we didn't belong together. I didn't want to look different. I wanted to be like any other kid in sixth grade, but I couldn't.

"Let's go ride bikes," I said.

"Where?" Matt asked.

"I don't know. To the creek?"

"Okay."

I like going to the creek at the end of our street, even though the water is cold. Matt and I raced down the street with a little brotherly competition. At the creek, we tried to skip stones across the water as far as we could. One, two, three jumps. It doesn't always work. You have to have the right kind of stone. The water always makes me feel more peaceful. Does it do that for everyone? If so, that's like a super power.

The creek looked bigger and deeper than before. Must have been because of the rain we got earlier in the week.

"Are Mom and Dad going to let you go to Newark?" Matt asked. He had heard my conversations with Mom and Dad.

"I don't know. It's not looking good right now."

"I hope they do," he said. "It would be cool if you get to visit your birth mom and your half-sister."

"Yeah. It seems like she wants to see me."

"Maybe she misses you," he said.

"Maybe."

"I miss my birth mom and birth dad."

"Yeah. I know. Maybe they'll call you someday," I said.

"Maybe."

"One time I dreamed that I was on a plane with my birth mom."

"Where were you going?" Matt asked.

"I don't know. I remember we had hotdogs on the plane. And the airport was kind of strange and orange. Not like it normally is. Did you ever dream something like that?"

"One time I dreamed I was in my classroom at school, and I turned around to look at the teacher, and the teacher was my birth mom," Matt said.

"How did you know it was her?" I asked.

"I just knew. Everything seemed mostly normal, except the other students weren't there. Just me."

"Did you ask her anything?"

"I can't remember," he said. "She was talking about math. It was multiplication. I knew the answers, and I kept drawing weird things with markers on my desk. And the classroom had a giant trampoline." We laughed.

"That's a good dream, bro. You want to get out of here?"

"Sure."

We rode our bikes home. The sun was high and bright. The mail truck passed by, and I waved to the mailman. He always waves back. The two Cocker Spaniels in our neighbor's yard rushed to their fence and barked loudly at the mail truck. Our next-door neighbor was cutting his grass and listening to music on his headphones, just like he does every week. So many familiar sights and sounds. It was comforting.

CHAPTER

THIRTEEN

SOON WILLOW WILL have to take a test to see if she's suitable to become a service dog. I didn't want that day to come. I didn't want her to leave us.

By mid-October, our lacrosse team's record was 5-2. I was enjoying our practices twice a week, and we kept improving. Our teamwork and passing were getting better. We still needed to work more on our shooting. Our defense was always been better than our offense, if you ask me. Coach Sam started making us do more shooting drills in practice.

The bleachers were twice as full as usual at our games. More extended family and friends of the players showed up at our games, wearing their new wristbands, eager to see what would happen next. Nothing unusual happened, but we did have a lot of fun.

Our church had its monthly potluck, so we took Willow with us. She did a good job at not getting too distracted by all the people. She was content to stay by my side and not rush over to greet people. But she made a few mistakes. She ate some crumbs off the floor and sniffed at my plate. I had to stop her before she took my biscuit. Dad said she needs plenty of practice to completely stop grabbing food.

Willow kept growing bigger and bigger. She was super-strong even when she wasn't fully grown. So strong that I couldn't always control her on the leash when she ran after a squirrel. But that didn't happen very often. She listened really well to me most of the time.

Everyone liked seeing her at church, especially the little kids. They scurried around her and got close enough to almost pet her, but stayed just out of reach. But I did have to remind one little girl not to pet Willow. A lot of the kids didn't have dogs at home, so it was exciting and fascinating and a little scary for them all at the same time. Willow tilted her head and seemed amused by them. Isn't it funny how dogs can be so human sometimes?

CHAPTER

FOURTEEN

I GOT TO TEXT with Imani a few times on Mom's phone. Just normal stuff about school and family and the holidays.

One day on the phone I asked her, "Why did you send me the postcard now, after all these years?"

She paused to think for second and replied, "Rayna keeps askin' 'bout you. She wants to know you. I don't know what to tell her because I can't answer most of her questions."

"Did she just find out about me?"

"Yeah, her dad told her a few weeks ago. I thought maybe she was too young for it."

Actually, I was glad he told Rayna. "It's good that she knows," I said.

In our text exchanges, Imani liked to hear about me, but usually when I asked her about herself, she stopped texting back. I didn't understand why. Was something wrong with what I said? Were my questions too personal?

Mom and Dad are thinking about giving me my own phone, which would be the all-time best Christmas gift ever. Unless it's a dumb flip phone. That's not cool.

Mom and Dad spoke with Imani privately a couple of times. They arranged for me and Mom to meet her on November 2 at a pizzeria about three blocks from her apartment in Newark. November 2 was two weeks away. I couldn't believe I had to wait two weeks. That's forever!

I was curious to see if I could remember being a baby. To get a glimpse of where I came from. The curiosity was making me restless and agitated.

Matt seemed strange, too. He kept picking fights with me over stupid stuff like where to sit in the car. He even hid my sneakers, so I had to spend 15 minutes looking for them and almost missed the school bus. This wasn't like him at all.

Over the next two weeks, we played two more lacrosse games. We won the first and tied the second, so our record was 6-2-1. On the lacrosse field, I was absorbed in the moment. Everything else went away. I didn't think about school work or my birth parents or chores or anything else. I liked that feeling.

It was hard to concentrate in school with so much going on. Who cares about polygons and calculating surface area, anyway? It's so boring. It's not like I'm going to use that stuff when I'm 30 years old. The good news is I got an A on that book report on Jim Brown.

During classes, I kept looking at my watch. October 25. More triangles and quadrilaterals. More homework. October 28. More science tests and labeling animal cell parts. October 29. It was going so slowly. I was barely thinking about Halloween at all. I'm probably too old to go trick-or-treating anyway.

Jalen invited me to a party at his house the day before Halloween. I dressed up as Steve Irwin, the crocodile hunter. He was a super-cool guy. I used to love watching his shows where he would wrestle crocks and cuddle koalas. But at the party, not once did I say "Crickey!"

That's not cool. Jalen was Groot from Guardians of the Galaxy. Demarcus was Black Panther, and he created a killer playlist for the party. I heard 50 Cent throwing down.

Catch me in a bad mood, flippin' you'll take a whippin'
animal, hannibal, cannibal addition
tears appear, yeah, blurring your vision
fear in the air, screaming, your blood drippin'

I sat down on a high stool in the kitchen and grabbed a handful of popcorn. Jalen's dad asked me about the blowup at the lacrosse game against Pasadena. He'd heard about it from some other kids, but he hadn't talked about it with me yet.

"Don't let those guys get you down on yourself, Carter," he said. "You can't control what other people say about you. But you can choose to ignore them and not believe their lies. Your race is one part of who you are, but don't let it restrict you or confine you."

"Did you ever get called names like that?" I asked.

He paused and thought about it. "Son, I've been around a long time, and I've heard a lot of hateful things directed at me and my family members. I can't say that it didn't hurt. But I tried to not let it infect my mind and poison my confidence."

I nodded thoughtfully. He smiled and gave me reassuring pat on the shoulder.

On Halloween, Matt dressed up as Spiderman and trick-or-treated with Mom. I stayed at home and handed out candy with Dad. It was pretty nice, actually. He was so happy to see all the kids and joke around with them. We ate popcorn and made bets on how many Princess Elsa costumes would arrive at our door in one night.

The closest guess earned the winner a jumbo bag of peanut M&Ms. I won, of course.

On November 1, Matt went to the school nurse with a stomachache and left school early. He got to snuggle with Willow, drink ginger ale and watch TV all afternoon. I thought he was faking. Mom said the stomachache was real, but how would she know?

Later that night, I laid in bed for a long time, but sleep wouldn't come. I checked my bag three times to make sure I had everything: postcard, address, socks, underwear, toothbrush. It was all there, safe and secure.

I hugged Willow close. Mom wouldn't let me bring Willow to Newark, which was disappointing. I kept trying to sleep. Willow's breaths got slower and slower. That made me feel sleepy. I finally drifted off, but I woke up super-early the next morning.

CHAPTER

FIFTEEN

AT 9 A.M., Mom and I dropped our bags in the trunk, ready to go to Newark. Dad and Matt stayed at home, since the visit with Imani would probably be easier and simpler that way. Plus, Matt didn't want to miss his soccer game. He didn't even wave goodbye when we left. Instead, he just turned around and got a soda from the fridge.

Mom and I drove the three hours to Newark, sometimes passing farms and later passing dirty industrial areas.

"It's a big day. Are you excited?" Mom asked.

"Yeah. But I'm nervous, too."

"Nervous about what?"

"I don't know. What if it's not a good reunion?"

Mom nodded, as if that all made sense, even though it didn't. "We don't know for sure how it will go, but I'm here for you, Carter, no matter what," she said.

"I know."

After two hours, my legs got so fidgety in the car. Luckily, there wasn't much traffic. I couldn't wait to get there.

Finally, we walked into the pizzeria, and my legs felt better. The smell of garlic and oregano filled the entire space. It automatically put me at ease.

We saw Imani sitting in a booth, wearing a black jacket and jeans and tall boots. Her hair was in very long, loose braids. They looked shiny and dark, like a lake at night.

We waved to her and sat down in the booth so awkwardly. We both had trouble deciding whether to sit next to Imani or across from her. Mom and I bumped into each other, and she accidentally stepped on my foot. So embarrassing.

Finally, we both took a seat across from Imani, and she shook hands with us. I was expecting Rayna to be there with her, but she wasn't.

"Hi," Imani said shyly. She was so soft-spoken that I almost couldn't hear her. It seemed like I wasn't the only one nervous about this meeting.

She looked so much like me, it was stunning. I had never felt that before. The main difference was her skin was a little darker than mine. She looked young, around 30. I think she was 19 when she had me.

Mom smoothed things over by talking about the sunny weather and our easy drive to Newark. I was grateful to her for being cool with all of this. It's a lot to take in, even if you're an adult.

"Where's Rayna?" I asked.

"She's with her dad," Imani said. "I wanted to talk with you on my own today, and maybe you can meet her another time."

I noticed Imani's big gold earrings, shaped in a circle. They bounced around when she talked.

Imani told us about moving to Newark last year to live with her sister and take a job as a preschool teacher. Before that, she worked at a small day care center in Maryland, but it closed when the owner retired. Imani lost her job and decided to move.

Her mom, Lynda, came to Newark about eight years ago to help Imani's sister, Kenya, take care of her kids after Kenya got divorced. Imani and Kenya have another sister who's younger. They're a close family. I could hear it in the way Imani talked about everyone.

Imani told us she would be spending Thanksgiving with her mom and Kenya in Newark. They planned to have a few friends come over for dinner. Our Thanksgiving would be at Uncle Brian and Aunt Laura's house, as usual.

Our pizza and mozzarella sticks arrived, along with water and Sprite. But I barely registered the taste of it. I was so fascinated by everything I was learning.

Imani asked me about my school and my friends. I told her about my lacrosse team and riding bikes with John after school and hanging out with everyone at the pool in the summer. I told her about one time at the arcade when I gave Jalen my ham sandwich and Skittles because he couldn't eat the pizza and ice cream everyone else was having. He's lactose intolerant.

She talked about being a shy kid who didn't have a lot of friends, but had a few really close friends from the school choir. Growing up, she felt like not many people knew her, but she could trust the few friends who were close.

"I didn't want people to see me as the poor kid. My mom couldn't afford things like camps and pool memberships, so I was pretty bored in the summer most of the time," she said.

Her favorite thing in the summer was singing in a musical theater group run by her church. They did *Godspell* and *Jesus Christ Superstar*. She sat up a little taller when she talked about music and singing. Her dark eyes looked full of energy and vibrancy.

"What about my birth dad? How did you meet him?" I asked.

"Ron. I met him at community college. We had a biology class together. He wanted to be a veterinarian."

So that's where my love of animals came from. It all makes sense.

"Is he a veterinarian now?" I asked.

"I think he's a vet tech, but I'm not sure." She looked downward and seemed uncomfortable talking about him.

"Carter, I left him because he drank too much and beat me up twice. That's why I decided to do the adoption. I was scared he might try to come back into my life and end up hurting the baby." She turned her head away and suddenly looked very young and small. I stayed quiet for a while, not wanting to intrude on her feelings. I wasn't expecting to hear all of this.

"Does he know about me?" I asked.

"Yeah. He signed the adoption papers. His grandma basically forced him to."

"Why did she do that?" I asked.

"She knew he couldn't be a stable daddy. He would be in and out, real great one week and real scary the next week. We kept askin' him to get help for his drinkin', but he wouldn't."

Imani paused and looked thoughtful. Maybe remembering something good.

"Boy," she said, stretching out the syllable slowly. "You know I loved that fool for two whole years. He had a great sense of humor. One time he threw a surprise birthday party for me and convinced all my friends to come to this roller skatin' place. He lip synched to all the sappiest love songs to make me laugh. His friend wore a red Michael Jackson jacket and kept tryin' to moon walk on skates. We laughed so hard we could barely stand up on those skates!"

Imani smiled and looked more relaxed.

"Ron brought Heath bars to share with everyone. Heath bars are my favorite."

"I love those, too," I said. Another connection there. Heath bars are my all-time favorite.

"I used to keep them in my bag to share with Ron after class. I know some folks went way out of their way just to go past my desk when they wanted some of that chocolate."

We both laughed. It felt like a lot of the blank spaces in my history were finally getting filled up. You know when you're doing a cross-word puzzle, and you get on a roll with one answer leading you to the next and the next? It was kind of like that.

Suddenly, Imani looked terrified. She quickly turned her head and grabbed her jacket and her purse. She put a $20 bill on the table. Was she trying to hide her face? I wasn't sure. Before I could get any words out, she was gone. No goodbye or anything.

Mom looked stunned. "Maybe she just had to go to the bathroom," Mom said, trying to appear hopeful, but something in her voice sounded seriously doubtful.

Two black men sat down at the table next to ours and ordered pizza. They seemed to be having a relaxed, friendly talk over lunch. After we waited for 10 more minutes, Mom started looking at her watch. No sign of Imani. No text or anything.

"Maybe we should text her?" I mumbled.

"Let's give her a little more time," Mom said with a concerned expression.

We sipped our drinks and sat there for another 20 minutes. Imani never showed up. My insides felt gutted. I tried to think about lacrosse drills, just so I wouldn't cry right there at the table.

I didn't understand what happened. One second everything was fine, and the next second she disappeared like a cat afraid of her own shadow. Mom texted Imani, but there was no response.

With nothing better to do, we drove all around Newark to look at the neighborhoods. We saw lots of skyscrapers and a river and some huge bridges. The city was crowded with lots of people who were shopping and walking and shouting at each other and honking their car horns. We saw a medical school and a law school.

There were homeless people with dirty signs, asking for food and money. There were moms pushing babies in strollers and young people sitting on the sidewalk and smoking. Everyone I saw was black or Hispanic. I liked the feeling of fitting in with the people around me, at least visually. It was an unusual feeling for me, but in a good way.

"Carter, are you doing okay?" Mom asked.

"Yeah, I'm okay," I nodded. "My birth mom left so quickly. Was it my fault?"

"No, it wasn't your fault. I imagine it's not easy for her to remember everything. But you know your dad and I will love you forever. We're your family forever." Her words and voice were reassuring and familiar.

"Love you, too, Mom," I replied. I stared out the window. The sky was getting grayer as nighttime got closer.

Eventually, we picked up sandwiches at Subway and drove to our hotel in silence. It was too early to go to bed. We had planned on being out later and didn't really know what to do with our time. Mom turned on the TV. Reruns of "The Office" were on, but we were only halfway watching. I was exhausted and sort of numb.

Around 9 p.m., Mom's cellphone rang, bringing us both out of our mental haze. Some anxiety started brewing in my stomach. It was Imani on the phone. She apologized for disappearing, explaining it was because she saw her pastor come into the pizzeria. No one outside of her family (except Ron and his grandma) knew about her pregnancy and the adoption. She said a couple of her friends were basically shunned by some folks at church after their teenage pregnancies, and she didn't want that to happen to her.

It all sounded lame to me. What's the point of hiding it now? Was I really that embarrassing to her? Again, I felt like I didn't belong to the black community, but also didn't belong to the white community. Maybe contacting Imani wasn't such a great idea. Coach Sam says to always be looking ahead for your next good move. But where was my next good move? I had no idea.

At the end of the call, Imani put her mother, Lynda, on the phone. Apparently, Imani had gone straight from the pizzeria to Lynda's house. Lynda invited us to have coffee at her home the next morning. I didn't want to go, but Mom sweet talked me into it by promising that we could get chocolate milkshakes on the way home.

CHAPTER

SIXTEEN

NOT FAR FROM our hotel was Lynda's small townhouse. It had a red brick path leading up to six front steps. Lynda opened her front door and said warmly, "C'mon in now. I'm happy to see y'all." She gave me a little sideways hug.

Lynda looked so much like Imani, just older. I could tell Imani got her wide-set, almond-shaped eyes from Lynda. With the same nose and almond-shaped eyes as them, I definitely looked related. Lynda had short, curly hair with golden tips.

Imani said a quick "hi" to us and fidgeted with her braids. She ushered us into the living room, which looked clean and comfortable, but not fancy.

Mom and I sat on an olive green couch next to a white bookshelf with lots of paperbacks and some religious books. Lynda set a tray with iced tea and chocolate chip cookies on an oval coffee table in front the couch. The coffee table and the bookshelf looked old and worn, but still holding up well. I grabbed two cookies.

"So I imagine y'all have lots of questions," Lynda said as she sat down in a beige upholstered chair that seemed a little too small for her. She's a pretty tall person. Maybe I'll be tall, too.

"I can tell you Imani was a strong little girl," Lynda continued. "Very athletic. Always climbing trees when she was your age. Sometimes I'd have to stand there for 10 or 15 minutes, trying to convince that girl to come down and eat lunch." She shook her head, looking both amused and exasperated.

I love climbing trees, too, especially the willow trees by the creek.

Lynda showed us some framed photos of the family celebrating Christmas and Easter and birthdays. Then she showed us a photo album full of snapshots of Imani as a baby, looking so tiny and round. Her mouth looked the same as mine does in my baby pictures. Two full lips, one small dimple above the upper lip.

"Do you have any pictures of my birth dad?" I asked.

"I probably do. Let me look," Imani said, scrolling through photos on her phone.

"Here's one." She showed me a picture of a guy with thick brown hair and a big smile, almost like he was about to tell a joke. His arm was wrapped around Imani's shoulders. He looked about two or three inches taller than Imani. There was something intense about his attitude.

"And you don't know where he lives right now?" I guessed.

"Nah," Imani said. "I heard he moved to Atlanta, but that was right before you were born. I ain't talked to him in a long time."

I stared at a stack of quilts that looked handmade, folded neatly next to the couch. They were all different colors: deep red, violet, light blue. One quilt mixed tan and navy blue. That was my favorite.

Lynda said with pride, "Imani made all of those quilts. She loves to quilt and knit. Used to take her knitting with her everywhere – church, basketball games, family birthdays, car trips."

"They're beautiful," Mom murmured softly.

I never knew anyone who could knit or sew things. I admired Imani for being able to make something like that so well with her own two hands.

"Can you tell us about Imani's dad?" Mom asked.

Lynda said, "He was a good father and an excellent electrician. He was born and raised in Maryland." She looked down and paused, taking a big breath. "He went to prison for 20 years for a stabbing he didn't do," she continued. "It was at a go-go show in Suitland. He missed most of Imani's childhood. He got out 10 years ago, and he passed away six months later from a stroke."

"I'm sorry. That must have been very hard for all of you," Mom said gently.

"Before they arrested him, we were doing really well, living in a nice townhouse in a safe neighborhood," Lynda recalled. "I imagined my girls growing up there, riding bikes and playing tennis and jumping in piles of leaves in the fall. After he went to prison, I tried to keep the townhouse, but after a year, we had to move to my mom's place in Landover. I wasn't making enough as a home health aide to stay where we were."

I pictured Imani and her sisters growing up without a dad to tuck them in at night. I felt grateful for all the times my dad was there to read Curious George stories to me, take me to the school bus stop or cheer for me at a lacrosse game.

"So you have three daughters?" Mom asked Lynda.

"That's right. Jordyn and her husband are in Pittsburgh now. They have two little boys in kindergarten." Lynda smiled and laughed. "They are jokesters, always teasing us. And Kenya is here. She has a boy and a girl, both in middle school. I make sure they study hard."

Her love for her grandkids made her face shine, taking on a beauty and energy I hadn't seen before. Her family meant everything to her. In the hallway, the walls were full of her grandkids' school portraits.

For a long time, we kept talking about our families. I felt I understood Imani a lot more, but I was still confused about something. What happened to Rayna's dad? I felt bad for her if her dad died or something like that.

"Is Rayna's dad here in Newark?"

"Yeah, he's here. He takes Rayna every other week. It didn't work out between me and her dad," Imani said.

I nodded. Like I said before, family is so complicated.

"Could you text me some pictures of you and Rayna?" I asked.

"Sure," Imani said.

I looked around, trying to memorize everything, like my eyes were a digital camera, capturing all the colors and shapes and textures in the living room. Mostly common, ordinary things like pink teacups and flowery wallpaper with a light green design. I took it all in. You never know what small detail might have meaning later. There were too many questions to ask.

I soaked in the smell of chocolate chip cookies – plus something else I couldn't name, something kind of lemony. Later, maybe it would remind me of Lynda. I only have one grandma, since my dad's mom passed away a few years ago. Maybe Lynda could be like an extra grandma to me. That wouldn't be too bad. Not bad at all.

I gave Lynda and Imani a big hug goodbye. I didn't know what to say, so I just said, "Bye." I felt kind of sad to leave, but also tired. I napped on the ride home.

CHAPTER

SEVENTEEN

MATT WAS SHOOTING basketballs in our driveway when Mom and I pulled up to our house later that day.

"Hey, bro," I said.

"Hey. How did it go in Newark?" Matt passed me the ball, and I took a shot.

"It went okay."

"You seem not as excited as I thought you'd be," Matt said. He missed his next shot, and he caught the rebound.

"Well, it wasn't really what I expected. My birth mom seemed different than I thought," I said.

"Why?" Matt tossed me the ball, and I made a lay-up.

"She disappeared when we were at the pizza place," I said.

"Really?"

"Yeah, it was stupid. She didn't want her pastor to see me. I wonder if she's a little unstable. But there were good parts, too, like hearing her stories and her laugh," I explained.

"Oh," said Matt. "Did you see your half-sister?"

"No, I didn't get to meet her. I'm hoping I can meet her later."

I missed my next shot, and Matt got the rebound.

"When I'm older, I'm going to find my birth mom and dad," Matt said. "I want them to come to my birthday party."

I blocked Matt's shot, but then I took it easy on him for the next one.

"My birth mom doesn't know where my birth dad is," I said. "I don't know if I'll ever be able to find him. They said he drank too much and hurt my birth mom."

Matt was quiet with a somber look on his face. I dribbled and passed the ball to him.

Mom came outside to take Willow for a walk. "Dinner will be ready in about 15 minutes, okay?" she called to us.

"Okay, Mom," I said.

Matt and I kept playing one-on-one for a while. We didn't need to talk more. We understood each other without a lot of words.

The more I thought about it, the more I sensed that things would probably not turn out the same for me and Matt as we look for more information about our biological parents. That's not fair at all. It's like a whole bunch of chapters of our history were taken away from us at birth. Nobody knows if Matt will ever be able to get those chapters back. At least I got the chance to start the ball rolling, kind of like getting through the first level of a video game. We'll see where it leads from here.

CHAPTER

EIGHTEEN

THE NEXT WEEK, the whole sixth grade went on a field trip to the Benjamin Banneker Museum in Catonsville. Our social studies teacher told us Benjamin Banneker was a free black man and self-taught astronomer, mathematician, surveyor and almanac writer. He owned a farm near Baltimore.

At 9:15 a.m., we all squeezed on to the buses like a big, mashed-up herd. We could hardly hear each other talk because the noise was so loud, which just made everyone shout louder. I sat next to John and gave him a look like "man, this is lame." He nodded.

The bus ride took 30 minutes, but felt like 150 minutes. It was bumpy and hectic. I was glad when it was over. We all had brown paper bags or plastic grocery bags for our lunches and drinks. I put mine in the front pouch of my hoodie. It was a little too heavy in there, but I kept it there anyway.

We all slogged into the museum slowly. Hanging on the museum walls were two huge quilts with symbols representing key parts of Benjamin Banneker's life, like farming, reading, his almanacs and the clock he created. These quilts reminded me of the quilts that Imani made.

In a smaller exhibit room, I read a quote on a plaque. Banneker was slamming Christians for supporting slavery! This guy was fierce. I was starting to really like him. He even helped to measure and map out the boundaries for Washington, D.C. before it was the country's capital.

A few kids from my class kept scrolling through social media on their phones, even though the chaperones kept telling them not to. A popular kid named Ian Jessup complained, "This is so boring. When can we get out of here?" He turned his head and thought the teachers didn't hear him, but I'm pretty sure at least one or two of them did.

I didn't think it was boring at all. But a lot of the kids were getting restless. Boys were fake punching each other, and girls were messing with their hair. One girl even pulled out a full makeup bag and started putting something on her eyelashes. So strange.

The teachers ushered everyone outside to a small cabin to watch how they cooked meals on Banneker's farm back in the 1800s. A guide showed us how they baked cornbread in a Dutch oven over a fire or hot ashes. She showed us the root cellar under the floor. It had carrots, potatoes, turnips and butter. It was smaller than I would have guessed. It looked a little too dusty for all that food to be down there. Not exactly appealing.

Back then, it must have been such a huge pain spending almost all of your time dealing with food and meals. It took practically all day, not like it does now with everything that we can buy in grocery stores today. After the demonstration, we didn't get to eat the old-timey food because there wasn't enough for all of us.

Looking at copies of pages from Banneker's almanacs, I could tell he was wicked smart, even though he didn't get to have a real education and good teachers. He taught everything to himself. I was a little surprised because every time you see slaves in textbooks and movies, they're always picking cotton or getting whipped. You don't see any other stories about their lives. Even the smartest ones didn't get a chance to learn much about the world outside the farm.

Luckily, Banneker was free his whole life. He easily could have been born a slave, and then maybe none of his accomplishments would have happened.

On the bus ride back to school, I sat next to John.

"Hey, man, you looking at that new girl, Alicia?" he teased, pointing his chin to indicate where she was sitting a few rows in front of us.

"No, man, it's not like that," I muttered with half a grin. "But she's not bad looking."

Jalen pulled his history notebook out of his backpack and said, "I kind of wish I had done my book report on Benjamin Banneker. That would have been more interesting than James Buchanan. Too late now, I guess."

After the field trip, Dad met me and Matt at the bus stop.

"How was the field trip, Carter?" Dad asked, sounding like he was in a cheerful mood.

"Good. Have you heard of Benjamin Banneker?" I asked.

"I don't remember much about his life," Dad said. "My history teachers might have glossed over him."

"He was a genius," I said. "Did you know he challenged Thomas Jefferson to end slavery? You should Google it."

Dad smiled. "Okay. I will." And he meant it.

We walked home, and after Dad finished his work emails, we played Uno for a while. I beat him, like I normally do.

"Save a game for me tomorrow, okay?" said Dad.

"Okay, Dad," I grinned.

CHAPTER
NINETEEN

A FEW DAYS LATER, a dog trainer named Stacey met us at the mall to do Willow's service dog test with Todd, who was going to become Willow's new owner. He lives in Maryland, close to the border with Washington, D.C. We met in the parking lot by the mall entrance.

Todd told us he used to be an Army infantryman, and his legs were injured in Iraq. Now he uses an power wheelchair and needs a service dog for certain things, like opening the refrigerator and retrieving the TV remote. He's an average-sized guy with big bicep muscles and a dark beard.

His power wheelchair was really cool. It can go 3.5 miles per hour and spin around in circles! He showed me how to put it into stand-up mode, too. That was awesome. Todd can do so many things that you wouldn't think he could do in a wheelchair, like play ping pong and lift weights.

Willow's test started out really well. She waited patiently and exited our car with control. Then she waited quietly in the parking lot. We walked through the Sketchers, TJ Maxx and American Eagle stores. Willow was so good. She didn't knock anything off the shelves or sniff any products. She sat when Mom asked her to, and she didn't lag behind.

She didn't even beg for food when we got some burgers and fries at Johnny Rockets. She sat quietly under the table while we dipped our fries in ketchup and sipped root beer. We didn't talk much, mostly because we were focused on Willow.

After lunch, it was time to take the elevator to the second floor of the mall. This would probably be Willow's hardest test. I knew she was nervous in elevators.

She entered the elevator with control, but when the elevator started moving, she started whining and looking around anxiously. She lowered her belly and shoulders toward the floor, as if that would make her safer. I saw the trainer taking notes. Mom gave me a slightly worried look.

Willow hesitated getting off the elevator and pulled hard on the leash for a few moments. My heart sunk. It took some time, but with a little encouragement, she got off the elevator, so we could walk past some clothing stores and a Starbucks that smelled sweet and bitter at the same time. I was glad Willow didn't make any mistakes there. It was just like we practiced many times before in various places.

When we finally got back to our car and let Willow inside, the trainer gave us the bad news. Willow failed the test because she was too scared of the elevator. I had no idea what would happen to her next.

"What if we go back and show you she can do the elevator?"

"Sorry, kiddo. I don't think we can do that today," Stacey said regretfully.

Mom frowned and asked, "So what do we do next?"

"I can help you work with Willow and see if she can overcome this fear of elevators. Let's see if some extra training helps over the next couple months," Stacey said.

Mom looked over at Todd and bit her lip, thoughtfully. I wondered what his life would be like without Willow. Stacey said he could get another service dog, but she wasn't sure when.

CHAPTER

TWENTY

MOM AND DAD invited Imani and Rayna to visit us on New Year's Day. Imani said she'd think about it and get back to us soon. I figured there was about a 50% chance that they would come. I wanted to show her my lacrosse trophies and my books.

Dad printed out some photos that Imani sent. One photo was of her and Rayna singing at church. Behind them were some beautiful stained glass windows showing trumpets and doves and a man reading a Bible. I couldn't stop staring at the bright colors in the windows. Imani's face looked joyful and alive. I kept the photos on my nightstand next to my bed.

We played our last lacrosse game of the season against a team from Sandy Spring. I thought about the whole crazy lacrosse season that started with a racist incident that no one will forget. Most of us players were a little taller and a little stronger now.

Jalen came to the game to root for me and John. My parents and John's parents were there, too. The game started out well with John scoring early in the first quarter. Chris had two lucky interceptions. We lagged a little bit in the second quarter, but managed to pull off a 12-10 win in the end.

I played pretty well, but John really had the game of his life. He ran faster than ever and scored with almost all of his shots. It was incredible! I was so happy for him. Jalen was in a great mood, thumping John on the back.

The three of us huddled near the pavilion next to the field. Jalen fist-bumped me. "Awesome game, man!" he said.

"Thanks, bro," I said. "Did you see that interception John made at the end?"

"Yeah. That was sweet!" Jalen agreed.

John grinned. We chugged Gatorade and soaked in the momentary feeling of victory. These things pass by so quickly, but I wanted to hold on to it and make it last. John took a selfie of the three of us.

As we talked, I realized was looking at two people who had known me my whole life. John and Jalen didn't see me as an adopted kid or a black kid. They saw me as Carter Young, their friend who kicks butt on midfield, loves dogs, and gets straight As in English. I felt connected and grounded and whole, more than ever before. It was a fantastic way to end the season.

CHAPTER

TWENTY-ONE

WILLOW DID FIVE training sessions with Stacey at different buildings that had elevators, including the library and the gym. Willow grew bigger, getting close to her full adult size. We took her to some new places to practice in between the sessions with Stacey. Unfortunately, she didn't lose her fear of elevators at all. She took another test and failed again. Mom and Dad had lots of discussions with Stacey about it. Stacey visited our house to deliver the final news. Willow couldn't continue in the service dog program.

I was sad for Willow, and I was worried about how she would feel if we gave her up. Wouldn't she be hurt and angry? Wasn't there some way on Earth for us to keep her?

"Well, dogs in training who don't pass the test still need good homes," Stacey said in a tone that meant she was suggesting something.

I felt a jolt of excitement in my neck and shoulders. "Mom, can we adopt her?" I blurted out, super-fast. I was on the verge of jumping up and down!

"Well, let's talk with Dad about it. Don't get your hopes up too much yet. It's a lot of responsibility to own a dog." Mom smiled her biggest smile and gave Willow a soft pat. Willow wagged her tail.

I groaned loudly. Adults are always making stuff way too complicated with boring things like responsibility and expenses and chores. It was so simple: Willow wanted us, and we wanted her.

"Do you think Dad will say yes?"

"Maybe," Mom said. "We'll see." She looked a little bit excited at the thought of adopting Willow.

For two weeks, we had many family debates about whether to adopt Willow. Matt and I lobbied hard to keep her. I even washed the dishes without complaining, and Matt gave Mom his "puppy dog" eyes, which works more often than you might think. He was wearing his purple Ravens jersey, which somehow made it even cuter.

Dad was hesitant, but I knew he loved Willow as much as the rest of us did. Since we were Willow's foster family, he wasn't planning on keeping her forever.

"It's a lot of time and money to take care of a dog. You're pretty busy with your homework and lacrosse," Dad said.

"But the lacrosse season is over. I swear I'll walk her every day when I get home from school," I pleaded.

In the end, Mom and Dad said we could adopt Willow, as long as we agreed to foster another service puppy later. That sounded perfect to me. I hated the thought of saying goodbye to Willow. She is part of our family. I knew that a long time ago, when I first looked at her and felt my heart open up more than the whole wide sky.

When Mom called Stacey and told her that we were keeping Willow, I was bursting with joy! It was like joy was coming straight out of my fingertips and toes. I picked up Willow and whirled around with her in a victory dance.

Matt ran down the street to tell his friend, Eddie Smith. He and Matt have been hanging out almost every day. I don't know why, but Matt's been a lot nicer to me since he and Eddie started hanging out. I think Eddie has a lot in common with Matt and me because he's adopted, too. Eddie knows that families are built out of love, not blood. Plus, Eddie likes seeing the Ravens win as much as Matt does.

The next day, Imani called to say it wasn't possible to visit on New Year's Day, but she could bring Rayna for a visit at our house in February. I was disappointed. Waiting really stinks.

Before they adopted me, Mom and Dad were on a wait list for a whole year. They waited for a year for Matt's adoption, too. Can you imagine doing that twice? It seems impossible.

At least I get to text with Imani sometimes, and I got a really nice Christmas card from Lynda with a family holiday photo. I taped it to our refrigerator to stay up there all year long. I can see Lynda and Imani and Rayna when I get a glass of milk or a cheese stick for a snack.

I asked Mom if she could take me to the store to get a present for Rayna. I got her a DIY kit for making your own unicorn pillow. It sounded like something fun she could do with her mom. I can give it to her when she visits us.

Eddie gave Matt a Megalodon nerf gun for his birthday, and Matt even let me borrow it so we could all have an epic nerf battle together. By the end, we were all so happy and spent that we collapsed on our couch in one big pile of laughter.

That night, I laid on my bed, listening to music. A familiar rap song started playing on Pandora. I knew the lyrics well.

I'm more than my successes. I'm more than my failures.
You'll see.
I'm not a demographic. Don't tell me what I can be.

I felt the strong beat, building and building. I kept concentrating on how that beat echoed inside my chest. When the song ended, I closed my eyes and smiled, trying to make the song last longer.

I started thinking about how there's a lot of positive things that come with my black heritage, along with all the difficult and painful parts. There's Benjamin Banneker and Jim Brown and my favorite sweet potato pie. Nothing's better than that.

It made me feel like I can love both sides of myself. I don't have to pick one side or divide myself in two. Maybe my two sides are like two powerful rivers, merging into one giant sea, knowing they are one. The rivers are not afraid. I am not afraid.

ABOUT THE AUTHOR

Leah Shepherd is a writer and yoga teacher who lives in Maryland with her husband and two adopted sons. She previously co-authored a nonfiction book called "The Three R's of Employee Benefits." Outside of yoga, her happy place is dancing, hiking or enjoying a captivating book.